...tter, to improve **BELLICOSE:** adj. aggressive, warlike, ready to fight **CACOPHONY:** n. a collection of harsh sounds **CAPTIVATE:** v.
ct of moving one's feet or body rhythmically **DEDICATION:** n. complete devotion, or an inscription in a book **DIMINISH:** v. made
adj. physically weak from age or sickness, frail **FONDLY:** adv. lovingly or affectionately **FROLIC:** v. to play in a light-spirited
cts, feelings and experiences known by a person **LAWN:** n. a stretch of open, grass-covered land near a house **LOLLYGAG:** v. to
ple color **MINUSCULE:** adj. very small **MOONLIGHT:** n. the light of the moon **NOURISHED:** adj. ... that is necessary
a **OPULENT:** adj. wealthy, rich, abundant **PENULTIMATE:** adj. next to the last **QUEST:** n. ... ...tion undertaken
E: v. to put a sword or dagger into a case **SHINNY:** v. to climb a rope or pole using ... ...NCERELY:** adv.
id, magnificent, fine **UNSATISFACTORY:** adj. not meeting your demands, inadequate, una... ... adj. devouring or
v. to sharpen, to make keen or eager **ABSCOND:** v. to leave in a sudden, secret ... ...ECTIONATELY:** adv. in a
HONY: n. a collection of harsh sounds **CAPTIVATE:** v. to attract and hold interest **CREATI...** ...adj. having the power of original
devotion, or an inscription in a book **DIMINISH:** v. made to seem smaller **ENCHANTMENT:** n. a magic spell **EPISTEMOLOGY:** n.
gly or affectionately **FROLIC:** v. to play in a light-spirited manner **GUTTER:** n. a channel for removing surface water **HALE:** adj.
of open, grass-covered land near a house **LOLLYGAG:** v. to hang around with no purpose **MAGNIFICENT:** adj. impressive in ap-
moon **NOURISHED:** adj. supplied with what is necessary for life, health and growth **ONOMATOPOEIA:** n. a word for a sound that
e last **QUEST:** n. an adventurous expedition undertaken to obtain something **ROOTED:** adj. having roots, firmly planted **SCINTIL-**
r pole using your shins and ankles **SINCERELY:** adv. in a manner that is genuine **SMILE:** v. to indicate pleasure by turning up
dequate, unacceptable **VORACIOUS:** adj. devouring or craving food in large quantities, or very eager **WEARY:** adj. tired, physi-
manner **AFFECTIONATELY:** adv. in a loving manner **AMELIORATE:** v. to make or become better, to improve **BELLICOSE:** adj. ag-
E: adj. having the power of original thought **CUISINE:** n. a style of cooking **DANCING:** n. the act of moving one's feet or body
a magic spell **EPISTEMOLOGY:** n. theory of the origin, nature and limits of knowledge **FEEBLE:** adj. physically weak from age
removing surface water **HALE:** adj. healthy **HARDY:** adj. sturdy or strong **KNOWLEDGE:** n. the facts, feelings and experiences
MAGNIFICENT: adj. impressive in appearance, extraordinarily fine **MAUVE:** n. a pale pinkish-purple color **MINUSCULE:** adj. very
OPOEIA: n. a word for a sound that is spelled like it sounds **OOLONG:** n. dark tea grown in China **OPULENT:** adj. wealthy, rich,
having roots, firmly planted **SCINTILLATING:** adj. animated, vivacious, witty and clever **SHEATHE:** v. to put a sword or dagger
v. to indicate pleasure by turning up the corners of your mouth **SPLENDIFEROUS:** adj. splendid, magnificent, fine **UNSATISFAC-**
r very eager **WEARY:** adj. tired, physically or mentally exhausted by hard work **WHET:** v. to sharpen, to make keen or eager
tter, to improve **BELLICOSE:** adj. aggressive, warlike, ready to fight **CACOPHONY:** n. a collection of harsh sounds **CAPTIVATE:** v.
ct of moving one's feet or body rhythmically **DEDICATION:** n. complete devotion, or an inscription in a book **DIMINISH:** v. made
adj. physically weak from age or sickness, frail **FONDLY:** adv. lovingly or affectionately **FROLIC:** v. to play in a light-spirited
cts, feelings and experiences known by a person **LAWN:** n. a stretch of open, grass-covered land near a house **LOLLYGAG:** v. to
color **MINUSCULE:** adj. very small **MOONLIGHT:** n. the light of the moon **NOURISHED:** adj. supplied with what is necessary for
OPULENT: adj. wealthy, rich, abundant **PENULTIMATE:** adj. next to the last **QUEST:** n. an adventurous expedition undertaken to
v. to put a sword or dagger into a case **SHINNY:** v. to climb a rope or pole using your shins and ankles **SINCERELY:** adv. in a
agnificent, fine **UNSATISFACTORY:** adj. not meeting your demands, inadequate, unacceptable **VORACIOUS:** adj. devouring or crav-
n, to make keen or eager to attract and hold interest **CREATIVE:** adj. having the power of original thought **CUISINE:** n. a style
a book **DIMINISH:** v. made to seem smaller **ENCHANTMENT:** n. a magic spell **EPISTEMOLOGY:** n. theory of the origin, nature and
o play in a light-spirited manner **GUTTER:** n. a channel for removing surface water ... ...DY:** adj. sturdy or
near a house **LOLLYGAG:** v. to hang around with no purpose **MAGNIFICENT:** adj. imp... ...ce, extraordinarily
plied with what is necessary for life, health and growth **ONOMATOPOEIA:** n. a word fo... ...is spelled like it sounds
enturous expedition undertaken to obtain something **ROOTED:** adj. having roots, firmly planted S...LLATING:** adj. animated,
ns and ankles **SINCERELY:** adv. in a manner that is genuine **SMILE:** v. to indicate pleasure by turning up the corners of your

THE Word Burglar

CHRIS CANDER
Illustrations by Katherine Tramonte

bright sky press
HOUSTON, TEXAS

bright sky press
HOUSTON, TEXAS

2365 Rice Blvd., Suite 202,
Houston, Texas 77005

10   9   8   7   6   5   4   3   2   1

Library of Congress Cataloging-in-Publication Data
Cander, Chris.
The Word Burglar / Chris Cander ;
illustrations by Katherine Tramonte.
      pages cm
Summary: When his family discourages reading and learning,
Word Burglar becomes angry and steals words from bedtime books.

ISBN 978-1-936474-96-7
[1. Reading–Fiction. 2. Learning–Fiction.]
I. Tramonte, Katherine, illustrator. II. Title.

PZ7.C161665Wo 2013
[E]–dc23   2012046415

Editorial, Lucy Herring Chambers
Creative, Ellen Peeples Cregan
Printed in Canada through Friesens

When he was quite young, the Word Burglar desperately wanted to learn to read. But his mother and father and brothers and sisters were too busy to teach him.

"Please," he begged. "The words look good enough to eat. Please, somebody! Teach me how to read!"
But no one ever did.

In the Word Burglar's small house, he was the smallest of the children, and the quietest. While his brothers and sisters grappled for dinner scraps and slivers of space on the bed, the Word Burglar just stopped trying.

He ate very little, he found nothing to be funny or fun, and he even stopped playing. So instead of growing, he diminished. While his siblings became hardy and hale, he shrank to the size of a well-sharpened #2 pencil.

Ignored by his family and starving for learning, the Word Burglar turned to a life of crime. By day, he slept unnoticed in a corner he shared with dust bunnies and old socks. By night, he crawled past the sleeping creatures in his crowded house and slipped under the neighbors' windowsills into their darkened bedrooms.

He noticed that many people read before bedtime. When their eyes became thick with sleep, they laid their books open on their nightstands, not even bothering with bookmarks, before they turned off the lights. He liked to creep under these tents and gaze at all the words. The curves and lines of their letters looked so beautiful. He longed to know their meanings.

One day, he found a pair of scissors belonging to his youngest sister's doll. He whetted them until they were as sharp as carving knives. That night, when he stole away, he sheathed them against his belt.

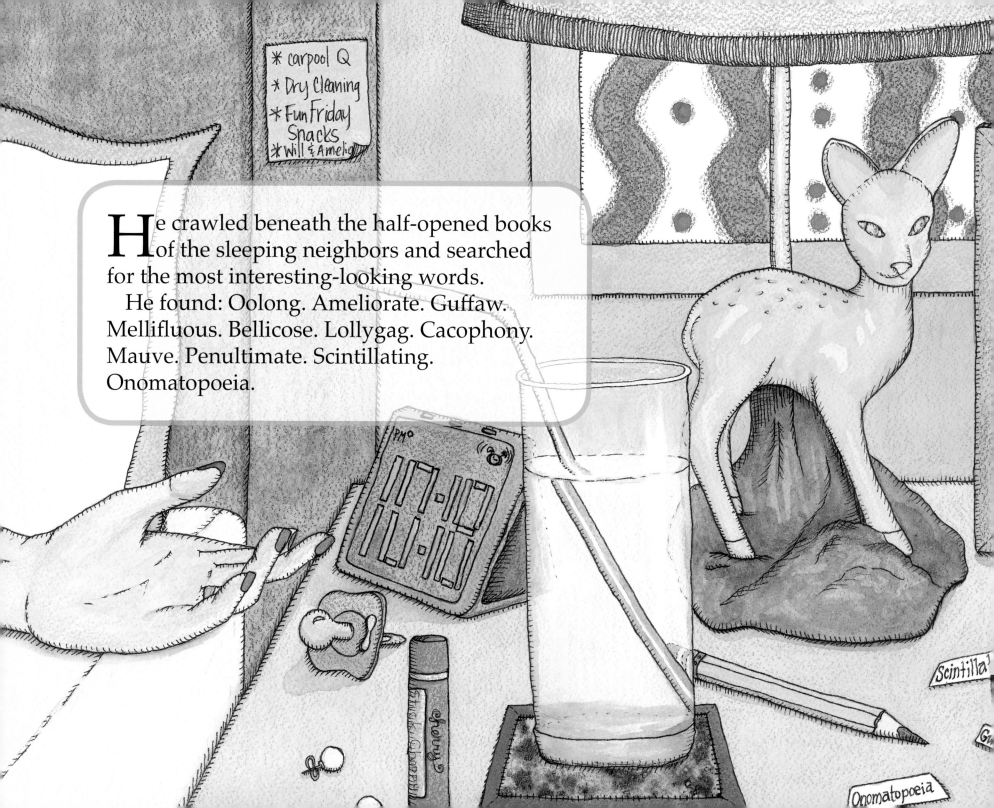

He crawled beneath the half-opened books of the sleeping neighbors and searched for the most interesting-looking words.

He found: Oolong. Ameliorate. Guffaw. Mellifluous. Bellicose. Lollygag. Cacophony. Mauve. Penultimate. Scintillating. Onomatopoeia.

* carpool Q
* Dry Cleaning
* Fun Friday Snacks
* Will & Amelia

He found small words in large books, and large words in small books, all of them equally captivating. Oh, how he cut and cut and cut, precisely and carefully, around them. He mangled sentences and spoiled paragraphs and ruined entire pages. Stories were suddenly meaningless because of the holes the Word Burglar left behind.

"I will make the biggest dictionary in the world," he thought. "And someday, I'll learn how to read all of it." He stashed his snaffled words in a messenger bag, which he slung across his narrow shoulders. When he returned home, he glued them neatly into an old math notebook his biggest brother had dropped beneath the bed. Night after night, he cut and pasted, and his dictionary grew fat. He, however, continued to shrink, because he still didn't know how to read.

More than once, when he became weary with hunger or thirst, he was forced to eat some of his words. "Cuisine" was the first to go. The words nourished him, and he felt a little bigger.

One night when he was feeling particularly small, he twisted himself into the room of a little girl named Sasha. She was a voracious reader and had dozens of books on her shelf. The Word Burglar didn't know that after she finished reading for the night, she lay awake thinking of all the magnificent stories in her books.

He shinnied up onto her nightstand and went right to work. Just as he was trimming the edge around the word *lawn,* a sweet voice rose above the clipping:

"What are you doing?"

The Word Burglar froze. A shaft of sudden lamplight sent him into a frenzy of blinking.

"N-n-n-nothing," he said, squeezing into the gutter between the spoiled pages.

"You were doing more than nothing," Sasha said. "You were taking the words right out of my book. Look!" she said, pointing. "Unsatisfactory. Feeble. And what's that one? Gutless."

The Word Burglar hung his head in shame.

"Why are you stealing my words?" Sasha asked.

The Word Burglar lifted his chin. "I'm making a dictionary. Someday I'll know how to read and spell all the words in the world!"

"But if you steal words out of books, then nobody gets to enjoy them. Why don't you just read them instead?"

"I don't know how," the Word Burglar said in barely a whisper. "Nobody ever taught me." Quietly, he began to cry. "That's why I feel so small."

Sasha looked at the miniscule boy on her bedside table. She looked at the words that lay in heaps at his feet. For a while, neither of them said anything. Then Sasha spoke.

"I'm a good reader," she said. "If you promise to stop stealing other people's words, I'll teach you how to read your own."

That very night, Sasha gave the Word Burglar his first lesson. He paid close attention to everything she said about the lovely letters and the sounds they made. By the time the cock crowed, not only could he read quite a few words, but he also stood taller and felt smarter.

"Will you teach me again, Sasha?" he asked.

"Only if you return the words you took," Sasha said. "Books are precious and powerful. They can make us stronger—especially when we share them."

The Word Burglar took his dictionary and carefully removed all the absconded words. It took several days, but he returned each noun, verb, adjective and adverb to its rightful paragraph.

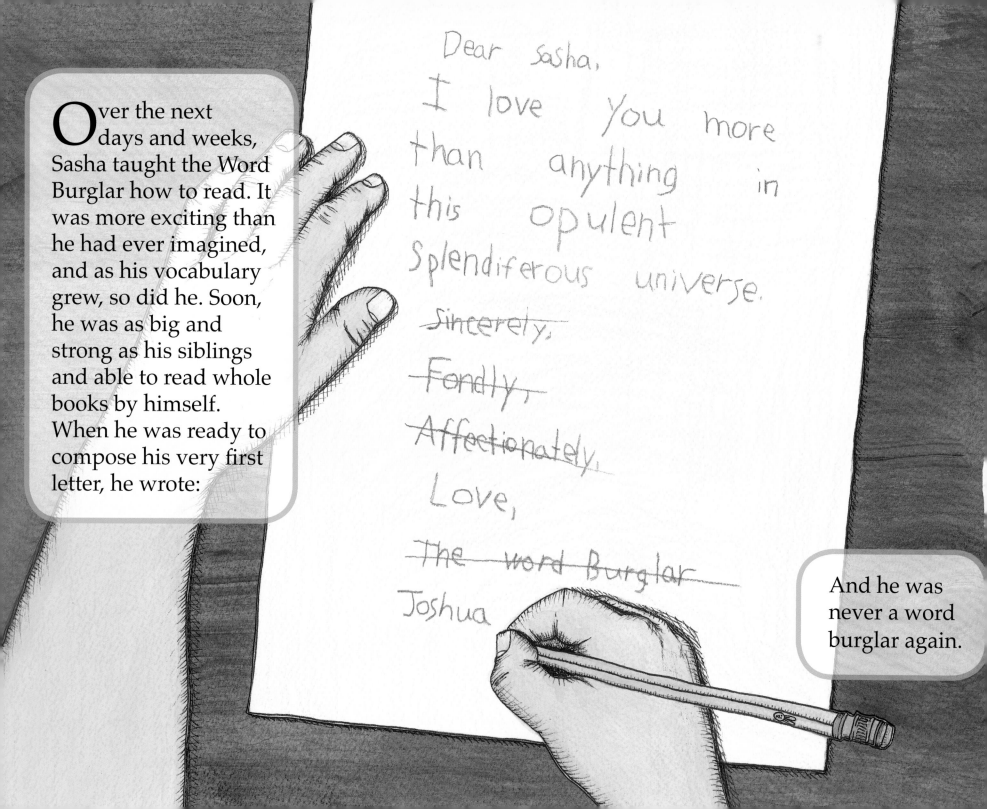

Over the next days and weeks, Sasha taught the Word Burglar how to read. It was more exciting than he had ever imagined, and as his vocabulary grew, so did he. Soon, he was as big and strong as his siblings and able to read whole books by himself. When he was ready to compose his very first letter, he wrote:

And he was never a word burglar again.

ABSCOND: v. to leave in a sudden, secret manner AFFECTIONATELY: adv. in a loving manner AMELIORATE: v. to make or beco
to attract and hold interest CREATIVE: adj. having the power of original thought CUISINE: n. a style of cooking DANCING: n.
to seem smaller ENCHANTMENT: n. a magic spell EPISTEMOLOGY: n. theory of the origin, nature and limits of knowledge FE
manner GUTTER: n. a channel for removing surface water HALE: adj. healthy HARDY: adj. sturdy or strong KNOWLEDGE: n.
hang around with no purpose MAGNIFICENT: adj. impressive in appearance, extraordinarily fine MAUVE: n. a pale pinkish
for life, health and growth ONOMATOPOEIA: n. a word for a sound that is spelled like it sounds OOLONG: n. dark tea grown in
to obtain something ROOTED: adj. having roots, firmly planted SCINTILLATING: adj. animated, vivacious, witty and clever S
in a manner that is genuine SMILE: v. to indicate pleasure by turning up the corners of your mouth SPLENDIFEROUS: adj. s
craving food in large quantities, or very eager WEARY: adj. tired, physically or mentally exhausted by hard work
loving manner AMELIORATE: v. to make or become better, to improve BELLICOSE: adj. aggressive, warlike, ready to fight
thought CUISINE: n. a style of cooking DANCING: n. the act of moving one's feet or body rhythmically DEDICATION: n. comp
theory of the origin, nature and limits of knowledge FEEBLE: adj. physically weak from age or sickness, frail FONDLY: adv.
healthy HARDY: adj. sturdy or strong KNOWLEDGE: n. the facts, feelings and experiences known by a person LAWN: n. a str
pearance, extraordinarily fine MAUVE: n. a pale pinkish-purple color MINUSCULE: adj. very small MOONLIGHT: n. the light of
is spelled like it sounds OOLONG: n. dark tea grown in China OPULENT: adj. wealthy, rich, abundant PENULTIMATE: adj. next
LATING: adj. animated, vivacious, witty and clever SHEATHE: v. to put a sword or dagger into a case SHINNY: v. to climb a r
the corners of your mouth SPLENDIFEROUS: adj. splendid, magnificent, fine UNSATISFACTORY: adj. not meeting your demand
cally or mentally exhausted by hard work WHET: v. to sharpen, to make keen or eager ABSCOND: v. to leave in a sudden, s
gressive, warlike, ready to fight CACOPHONY: n. a collection of harsh sounds CAPTIVATE: v. to attract and hold interest CR
rhythmically DEDICATION: n. complete devotion, or an inscription in a book DIMINISH: v. made to seem smaller ENCHANTME
or sickness, frail FONDLY: adv. lovingly or affectionately FROLIC: v. to play in a light-spirited manner GUTTER: n. a channe
known by a person LAWN: n. a stretch of open, grass-covered land near a house LOLLYGAG: v. to hang around with no purp
small MOONLIGHT: n. the light of the moon NOURISHED: adj. supplied with what is necessary for life, health and growth ON
abundant PENULTIMATE: adj. next to the last QUEST: n. an adventurous expedition undertaken to obtain something ROOTED:
into a case SHINNY: v. to climb a rope or pole using your shins and ankles SINCERELY: adv. in a manner that is genuine SM
TORY: adj. not meeting your demands, inadequate, unacceptable VORACIOUS: adj. devouring or craving food in large quantiti
ABSCOND: v. to leave in a sudden, secret manner AFFECTIONATELY: adv. in a loving manner AMELIORATE: v. to make or beco
to attract and hold interest CREATIVE: adj. having the power of original thought CUISINE: n. a style of cooking DANCING: n.
to seem smaller ENCHANTMENT: n. a magic spell EPISTEMOLOGY: n. theory of the origin, nature and limits of knowledge FE
manner GUTTER: n. a channel for removing surface water HALE: adj. healthy HARDY: adj. sturdy or strong KNOWLEDGE: n. t
hang around with no purpose MAGNIFICENT: adj. impressive in appearance, extraordinarily fine MAUVE: n. a pale pinkish-
life, health and growth ONOMATOPOEIA: n. a word for a sound that is spelled like it sounds OOLONG: n. dark tea grown in Cl
obtain something ROOTED: adj. having roots, firmly planted SCINTILLATING: adj. animated, vivacious, witty and clever SHEA
manner that is genuine SMILE: v. to indicate pleasure by turning up the corners of your mouth SPLENDIFEROUS: adj. splendi
ing food in large quantities, or very eager WEARY: adj. tired, physically or mentally exhausted by hard work WHET: v. to s
of cooking DANCING: n. the act of moving one's feet or body rhythmically DEDICATION: n. complete devotion, or an inscriptio
limits of knowledge FEEBLE: adj. physically weak from age or sickness, frail FONDLY: adv. lovingly or affectionately FROLI
strong KNOWLEDGE: n. the facts, feelings and experiences known by a person LAWN: n. a stretch of open, grass-covered
fine MAUVE: n. a pale pinkish-purple color MINUSCULE: adj. very small MOONLIGHT: n. the light of the moon NOURISHED:
OOLONG: n. dark tea grown in China OPULENT: adj. wealthy, rich, abundant PENULTIMATE: adj. next to the last QUEST: n.
vivacious, witty and clever SHEATHE: v. to put a sword or dagger into a case SHINNY: v. to climb a rope or pole using your